MURDERS OF THE RATTLER

JB CLEMMENS

MURDERS OF THE RATTLER

ReadersMagnet, LLC

Murders of the Rattler
Copyright © 2022 by JB Clemmens

Published in the United States of America
ISBN Paperback: 978-1-957312-21-7
ISBN eBook: 978-1-957312-20-0

All rights reserved. No part of this publication may be reproduced, stored in a retrieval system or transmitted in any way by any means, electronic, mechanical, photocopy, recording or otherwise without the prior permission of the author except as provided by USA copyright law.

The opinions expressed by the author are not necessarily those of ReadersMagnet, LLC.

ReadersMagnet, LLC
10620 Treena Street, Suite 230 | San Diego, California, 92131 USA
1.619. 354. 2643 | www.readersmagnet.com

Book design copyright © 2022 by ReadersMagnet, LLC. All rights reserved.
Cover design by Kent Gabutin
Interior design by Renalie Malinao

CHAPTER ONE

The voice frequency tabulator was invented when a choral singer used the company computer to work on improving the sound of his voice, especially pitch. The computer matched the frequency and sound of famous singers, duplicating them in output comparing them to the inventor's voice. There are unusually talented people who have this ability to duplicate singing voices without a computer.

Ceiling lights shone upstairs in Angel Sound Technology's computer center obliterating the darkness through the windows. The man inside compared two recordings and the Voice Frequency Tabulator found a match, but he shook his head. They couldn't be identical – one voice was his.

He stepped into the hall where a young man was finishing emptying trash. The older man was willing to work overnight on this project, but knew that Harry needed to go home very soon. He walked up to Harry and tapped on his shoulder. The young man's upper body twitched then relaxed when he saw who it was.

"I didn't see that coming, Mr. Trumble. I'm about finished here. Outside of security, we're the only ones in the building. Do you need something?"

Tom Trumble stood close and spoke slowly, enunciating each word.

"Would you come over to the computer room for something I'm working on now? I know your shift's almost over. It won't be very long."

"Oh, I see," Harry responded trying to mask his enthusiasm present for anything computer. Tom led Harry inside to a microphone on the desk.

"I need you to use these words and speak them exactly into the microphone. The VFT is recording you." Tom handed a very short script to him.

"Uh… *I'm going to blow something up if this persists.*" The young man sought confirmation for a job well done. "Is that it?"

"Yes. Now watch this." Tom played the other recording of a deep voiced man using those words.

"Who is that?"

"It's someone who threatened a client of ours – not yet identified. That's what we need to do."

Tom continued, "What's upsetting is that the Voice Frequency Tabulator indicates a match both with your voice and mine earlier. That's just not possible. I expected it to match the words but not frequencies. Something is wrong."

"I don't know, sir. In my physics class, I learned frequencies have something to do with pitch. Could some other pitch be interfering in the machine's calculations?"

"Harry, that's a great thought. I'll turn up the filters."

Tom muted the human voices and then he heard it… a high pitched whine or buzzing sound on the threatening tape. Harry, however, did not. His unfortunate hearing impairment prevented it. Tom turned VFT to face Harry and explained what was happening. Looking up, he noted that the fluorescent lights were giving off the same pitch now. The VFT had matched that, not the voices. Harry picked up on that without neeeding explanation.

"Harry, I can't keep you longer. School tomorrow. Thanks for helping me. A phD bested by high school physics now. It's good education, there, though."

"I'm just glad I'm not going to be arrested for being the threatening caller. It'll make a good story for friends. See you tomorrow evening, Mr. Trumble. Bye."

Tom waved and settled in to make modifications to the tabulator. He wrote a note to David, the CEO, informing him that the culprit here must work somewhere using fluorescent lights so probably not a just a homeowner. He shut everything down, wishing he could find a way to improve Harry's life and hearing. Such a smart and enjoyable kid.

CHAPTER TWO

The VFT's first success was identifying a caller to a nearby church. Threatening messages included *"You're dupes of religion"* and more intensely, *"All we like sheep have gone astray, you're just sheep now deserving of slaughter."*

The church secretary got alarmed enough to call police in to investigate. The only clue they found was that it was a fairly young voice. They, in turn, called on Angel Sound Technology to run voice identification and find matches. Robin Winger, a receptionist hired at the firm's opening told them, "We need tapes from various church services for comparison, probably even old ones that are available."

The secretary found several recordings and sent them.

The VFT used these criteria for identifications:

- Changes in dynamics
- Stress on syllables
- Pitch fluctuation
- Breathing times or breaks
- Lengths of word endings

MURDERS OF THE RATTLER

Of those recordings surveyed, only one of them matched from a Chritmas paegant eight years back. The word "sheep" exactly matched the caller's "sheep." Other factors matched very well too.

They had him and found his name, now a college sophomore at Berkeley. The minister offered to go there and speak to the boy who hadn't yet acted on his pent-up rage. Law enforcement advised against it so they contacted local police in California to pick the kid up for questioning.

AST's part over, they moved on. David Ellison, founder and CEO, was pleased with the conclusion of this first case, not knowing their next involvement would be identifying a murderer.

***

On a New York City side street near Light of Hope Mission, the Rattler had no trouble finding the homeless man named Rigoletto. He held out the Seiko to him and asked how he got to be homeless, though he already knew. The guy's story confirmed that he had found the right person. Through feeling of rage filled his mind, he suppressed it and unemotionally muttered "You're welcome" when Rigoletto thanked him for the Seiko. Around the corner, he threw a fist at the nearest trash barrel walking fast to his Toyota parked up ahead.

***

Robin, of Angel Sound Technology, had received tickets for a rare New York Philharmonic Singers concert of *Madame Butterfly*. A select few fans were invited to the recording session. Thrilled to attend, Robin read the tickets: *Sound system is sensitive – No applause. No noise from shifting seats, talking or eating.* Robin had acid reflux, resulting in burping, and took a pill to prevent that then she was off to the concert.

Up on stage, two men were talking in the wings.

"Fiona Mills is out tonight."

"It's fine. I've arranged for Violet Easton to replace her. She can imitate voices very well. See if anyone notices it isn't Fiona's voice."

The first man stepped onto the stage to remind the audience about the noise policy. Then the *Madame Butterfly Overture* started.

Only the Puccini opera music was being recorded, with no acting included. Robin followed the libretto for the story. Strains of *Star Spangled Banner* heralded Pinkerton's entrance. The orchestra played *"Tutti Zitti"* (which translates to "Quiet Everyone!") and the enlightened audience remained hushed through Violet's singing of *"Un Bel Di"* until…

They heard a boom, then the piercing sound of a woman's scream coming from the ground floor seats. Startled, the soundman stopped the recording immediately and the ushers raced to the row it originated from. A lady, very well dressed in expensive jewelry was sobbing. On her lap was a man, looking like an off-the-street, unkempt homeless type—eyes not moving, glazed upward… dead.

Though law enforcement recommends not moving the body, the woman was overwrought with grief. With the ushers' help, she extricated herself from the dead man's odious weight. A ticket stub fell from the pocket of the man's shoddy jacket. The patron's name on it was Bitsy Schwartz. The ushers recognized her as an important donor, and that Lieutenant Eli James of NYPD was her usual companion. So, they telephoned him. He got there fairly quickly, in his Cadillac, parking in Bitsy's regular space.

His first question rang out. "Who is the dead man?"

Ushers shrugged and no one responded.

He asked the familiar woman, "What exactly happened, Sophia? Are you harmed?"

"...James. He suddenly slumped over during the high notes of *Un Bel'Di* near the end."

"Then you screamed?"

"Finding a strange man in your lap, anyone would react to it that way."

"Of course, dear. I'm sorry this happened to you. It's understandable."

"Thanks. You know we're regular attendees in this row, as you and Bitsy usually are. My husband had duties elsewhere tonight. I wish he'd been here though."

James could understand why the unidentified man invading her space wasn't very pretty. Whatever happened, he died instantly. Because Sophia knew Bitsy and sat in their row, James arranged to have her auto delivered there to see her in safety to her home. He didn't need to telephone Bitsy for finding the reason this now dead man was holding her ticket. He did call to ask her to find Sophia's number and follow up on her emotional state. Of course he took a minute to explain things to his soul mate. Bitsy often gave tickets to homeless shelters, believing that music was important to everyone, low station or not. Only this poor unfortunate man paid with his life. Not a fair trade. The coroner arrived and began on the body.

"It seems something exploded on his arm. There are pieces of wristwatch embedded there. Cause of death is *vascular thrombosis*. While there are many normal conditions that might eventually cause clots, the explosion itself is a mystery."

"Was the victim fitted with a pacemaker or electronic device?" James asked.

"I don't know, but here is the shattered crystal of the watch in pieces. A bump on wood seats wouldn't cause that. It's almost as if something internal caused it to break apart. The broken glass face wouldn't have killed him though. I'll check for explosive residue and poisons back at the lab."

"The woman the victim fell on screamed at the end of an aria which is very high pitched. If pitch can break glass, it might have shattered the watch face and released something toxic," James surmised.

"It's possible. My van is outside and the attendants here can take the victim. I'll keep in touch."

Robin made her way to the stage. Even though the performance was interrupted she wanted to tell Fiona Mills that she'd enjoyed her singing. In the soloist's seat, however, was not Ms. Mills. A tall brunette stood and smiled up at her.

"You're not Fiona, yet I swear I recognized her voice singing *Un Bel Di*. I've heard her do it before. Sorry for lack of manners, I'm Robin Winger. I work for Angel Sound Technology."

"Hi, Robin. Sorry to confuse you. I'm Violet Easton and I'm to voices what Mel Blanc is to Bugs Bunny cartoons. Lou Rawls was easily able to cover songs, having that knack too."

"Quite fascinating, Miss Easton. I enjoyed hearing you. I might be stepping over boundaries, though I think you could help our company in many ways."

"What kind of company is it?"

"At Angel Sound, we identify voice patterns from electronic messages to match the callers, especially threatening ones, and solve crimes."

"Wow, sounds fascinating. Maybe you can even find out what happened to this guy in the audience. I heard he's dead."

"Really? I heard the sirens. I'll tell my boss all about it and while I'm at it, I'll see if he's interested in your unusual talent too. Our voice recognition software can identify voices but human singing is more difficult for it. I think my boss would be pleased to have you working with us. Would you be interested in that?"

"Only if it pays. I have the usual bills."

"Okay I'll ask him. He's really great."

Violet allowed herself to get excited at the possibility. She needed work and Robin's "offer" sounded promising.

CHAPTER THREE

David Edison was explaining the VFT to Violet. "From recording input, it selects certain words to compare. Are you familiar with keyword association?"

"Absolutely – drives most search engines."

"That's right. The VFT is quite efficient, keeping us from having to listen to entire recordings to match voice, or frequency of pitches. It selects sentences or idioms frequently used. Take the use of 'the' everyone uses it. The VFT would waste time comparing all recordings of it. It filters it out. Some infrequent words, though, recur and allow for good voice matching."

"What is the machine working on now?" Violet broke in.

"The incident at *Madame Butterfly* the other day."

"The only recording now for comparison is a call to Fiona Mills threatening her if she showed up to sing. There are tapes from the homeless shelter, too."

Violet spoke softly, tentatively, "Surely the victim didn't threaten the diva?"

"No, but he could have an enemy there."

"I don't understand it. What would Fiona's singing have stopped if the killer wanted to murder him?"

"That's what we need to find out. The murderer wouldn't intuitively have known you'd replace her. You sang the same notes. Although if pitch detonated the watch explosive, that's a consideration."

"Horrors! You think a pitch I sang caused the explosion that killed him?"

"I'm sorry to say, it's possible... though of course you did nothing wrong – and are not liable for it."

"Still, it's upsetting."

In an effort to distract Violet, David showed her their new challenging voice recording.

"This guy has a voice that would wake a very sound sleeper. Listen to it."

After the beep, a deep jittery voice said, *"Stop.Using.Paper. This is only a warning now, but soon I'll destroy and wreak havoc on your business if you ignore this—or me."*

The sound ended with one click but the verve lingered, sending chills to Violet's upturned arm hairs–impossible to separate what he said from the *insane* way he said it.

She inquired, "Have there been specific threats to one location?"

"It varies. One time a bomb threat... others, poisoning cafeteria food or... destroying a stockpile of papergoods."

"Terrible. Whoever he is, must be a *sicko*. How are you planning to identify him?"

"For now, looking for disgruntled employees previously recorded on company records. If you come to work for us now, that'd be something we could tackle together."

"Is that an official offer?"

"It is."

Violet did not miss a beat.

"Okay then I accept."

CHAPTER FOUR

Jake Arnold Glaxton left the ham radio on in the apartment, listening for call sign RT2666. He heard other people talking about things he considered nonsense—political opinions and women's recipe exchanges. He got up to use the bidet he'd installed, before sitting back in front of the computer again. His boyhood refuge appeared on the screen and he fought back the sadness. This photograph was the only one his Dad ever took and Jake had to beg him just to do that. His Dad never showed interest in him ever at all. In the picture, Jake was in the treehouse he built with his pet named 'Snidelee' and his Mom was at the bottom, singing up to him to call him to supper. No sound came out from the screen, but he could hear it clearly–'Zaccheus, you come down, for I'm going to your house today.' Only... no one protected his tree-house the next day when reckless, uncaring workers had destroyed it, including his pet. The thought of them caused overwhelming rage inside and he exhaled in a snarl.

Changing the visible screen to display of new credit card balance, it confirmed he now had thousands from profits of his ventures. He sold everything from 'How to care for your pet' information to 'Winners expected at the racetrack'. Expert advice on bonsai trees contributed too. He stood up and went to check on the trees in the other room.

"Breaker RT666, Empire Mill just raped the hell out of the woods next to my Dad's house. So somebody needs a piece of paper that bad to make birds find new location. Come back."

Jake responded angrily, while looking up Empire's phone number and entering their address in 'Reminders' on his computer. He wasn't even tempted to grab a piece of paper for it—no such thing in the apartment. Since he didn't have a conventional mailbox outside, he checked email. Nothing important except one from Theodore Barnes—" Testing of device resulted in a fatality. I quit."

CHAPTER FIVE

Violet was singing an old Elvis Presley hit as she listened for key words in the tape provided. Hoping *Jail House Rock* would further the search for the perpetrator or mastermind who had blown up a storage warehouse in the central Business District. So far... nothing. Violet noticed the informing message 'This is whoever's calling on a recorded line' was on almost every one.

Being recorded often made people nervous or sometimes speak louder. Some even take it as an opportunity to show off. Violet's motivation, however, was to find key phrases for the VFT to match exact sound with the deranged guy. The fact that there were recordings available didn't diminish the enormity of the task. The guy threatening to bomb storage areas had a low voice that rattled on some words. She was using his phrasing of "I'll shout from the treetops" for identifying a similar voice pattern. She found another one, "Sacrificed trees will vengefully ruin you." Analyzing by each word, "you" is common, "sacrificing" would only trigger things relevant to pagan rituals, so only "trees" or "treetops" might bring helpful information. She focused on those hoping to find the identity of the man.

Sometimes switching tasks improved clarity of the first task. Violet decided to change to the one which threatened Fiona Mills.

Using a somewhat high pitch for a man, the caller said, "For the performance of *Madame Butterfly*... I suggest you skip that. It's worth your while to consider canceling, not ignoring my advice with your elderly mother in a nursing home and all."

'So that's why Fiona bowed out of performing.' Violet nodded. 'The guy implied harm to her mother. We've got to get this *fiend*.'

For voice comparisons, there were tapes from the opera box office, and from the homeless shelter where the victim hung out. The stack of them was so daunting that Violet decided to eat lunch instead. She straightened up her desk and headed to the break room and refrigerator. Robin was already there eating and invited her to sit down.

"So great that you're working here. We have nobody here with an outstanding voice singing or speaking."

"Thanks Robin but your voice is pretty outstanding for answering the phone. I like being here. The atmosphere's tranquil." Violet noticed some potted plant nearby. "What is this tiny tree I'm sitting next to?" Violet gestured to it.

"It's a juniper bonsai, a gift from corporate headquarters. They said it's a reminder to nurture our clients as if caring for trees."

"I wouldn't know how to care for these. Is it specialized treatment?"

"At first I didn't either... so I called a specialist. He's kind of a weird guy but knows *everything* about bonsai. I have the recording of that around somewhere. I'll find that for you, if interested."

"That'd be great. I'm always excited to learn new things. Thanks, Robin!"

Violet took out her spinach when the microwave beep interrupted them. Though anxious to get back to the stack of tapes on her desk, she ate it slowly. Then tossing her vitamin water bottle in the nearest recycling bin she headed down the hall for work.

Listening to the first tape from *Light of Hope*, she heard a church elder promising food delivery. Not too surprising or important. A man's voice dominated the second time with intensity inquiring, "Is there any resident interested in *Madame Butterfly*? I have a ticket."

Now Violet was curious. It was a connection to this case.

"Well, that'd only be our one guy. What's your interest there?"

"As I said previously, I have a free ticket. I'd like to share it with an opera buff. It's worth your while to tell me the name." Violet stopped the tape and noted the date time stamp. The caller to Fiona Mills had used that *"It's worth your while"* expression.

"Guy's nicknamed 'Rigoletto'. Nobody knows his real name. Would you like to make a donation for our cause? We offer help to the homeless 24-7."

Violet noticed he hesitated then continued, "...I guess I could."

"Using a credit card is easiest way for you."

"Just one minute. Okay, here's the number - 6100 5555 4290 7310"

"What's the name on the card?"

The nervous voice hesitated again then answered, "Theodore Barnes." Violet was already entering the digits for police headquarters that David Edison gave her if she found important clues.

"How much did you want to get?"

"$35.00."

"Thanks very much, Mr. Barnes. You have a nice day."

After the recording ended Violet notified the boss and checked on police again, who acted on it immediately. They raced to Barnes's basement floor apartment and entered, breaking the unopened lock when they got no answer.

Lying on the floor inside was the lifeless body of Theodore Barnes. At first the coroner found nothing unusual. On closer inspection, two identical puncture wounds on the left leg, three inches apart, were observed under dried blood stains.

"It's a bite of some kind." George, the coroner, informed the police.

James responded, "It's not human, is it?"

"Most certainly not, teeth marks would be there. It's an animal. I'm guessing probably a snake from the fang marks evident."

"We're searching the apartment now, being very careful to avoid anyone else getting bitten if it's still here."

Finding no sign of a snake, Lieutenant James looked over the computer setup—very high-tech stuff, although smashed beyond use. It had included a sound wave analyzer and digitized recordings of chemical components.

"This guy had to have been some kind of scientist, technician or... maybe amateur sleuth."

"Whatever he was, it didn't save him," George responded grimly.

"That's true."

James turned over notes on the desk and found something interesting.

"There are scribbles here about pitch frequencies shattering crystal. I remember an old ad where a high soprano's singing volume shattered a glass. Do you know it?"

"Yes I do. I forget who the ad was for, though."

James' memory kicked in. "It was *Memorex*." He soon remembered the whole ad. "Proving that Ella Fitzgerald's voice could shatter glass, they cleverly showed that a tape recording of it could too, endorsing the sound quality of the cassette."

"There's more here about explosive devices detonated in that way. I think we've found our homeless man's cause of death... and the killer too. It's likely a substantial clue now, anyway."

"Is there anything that indicates why he did it?"

"No, not really."

"There's this slip of paper with Fiona Mills phone number. We know he threatened her, but if the intent was for her not to sing, it makes no sense… unless he was trying to stop it."

"Second thought?"

"He set things up for someone else, following orders."

"He was ordered to set up the killing but couldn't go through with it? And attempted interfering to prevent it." George summarized. "The snakes native to America are usually copperheads, king snakes and rattlers. From the fang marks, I'd say rattlesnake."

A knock on the door announced the police experts were now here.

In Mylar suits and helmets, they entered gruffly and kicked James and George out immediately. James thought they were acting a bit overdramatic, but then again, everyone's safety was important. A man had died from the rattlesnake encounter.

CHAPTER SIX

Even though the factory was twenty miles outside of the city, the putrid smell of the paper mill hung in the air near town. Violet noticed it right away, being sensitive, when the main sliding glass door was opened.

"What is that?" she asked, wrinkling her nose.

"That? That's the entrance door opening," chuckled a man nearby, about Violet's age. Violet appeared confused and the man restarted. "Oh, you mean new pulp scent? I'll explain if you want. You're Violet, aren't you?"

From her reception desk, Robin looked up, holding fingers to her nose.

"You haven't met our resident 'everything expert'. Violet, this is Tom Trumble. We call him Tom Thumb because he holds more knowledge in his thumb than the rest of us have in our brains."

"But I'm *modest*," replied Tom with a cheeky smile.

"He has a phD in neuroscience from the University of Pennsylvania and a master's from MIT... yet he has trouble opening packages of food."

"Now *who* doesn't," Tom protested. "I swear they glue them shut on purpose."

Violet moaned and groaned.

"It's even cruel sometimes when instructions indicate it's 'easy open'... *yeah right.*"

"I keep scissors handy at home, however at convenience stores, skill is required for fruit cups and chip bags…"

She placed the cardboard from her lunch food in the bin marked *"Recyclables'* and excused herself for going back to work. Tom agreed it was time to return and smiled broadly in Violet's direction saying, "Glad to have you here, Violet, and very nice talking to you. Hope our paths cross again soon."

She hoped that too, finding this Tom man quite interesting, and waved her hand back.

On the way to her desk, she thought about him, not self-absorbed as usual cerebral types were, but open, easy to talk to. He was interested in other people's opinions. She thought, 'an admittedly handsome type was just fine.

There was a package just delivered on her desk and she opened it – well attempted it. The carrier had used strapping tape which only slightly separated when she pulled on it. The strong fiber remnants cut into her hand. She chuckled, though, thinking of Tom's earlier mention about opening packages. She had a seven-in-one tool in the purse. Bottle opener, clippers, knife, screwdriver, inch measuring stick, scissors and nail file. Using the scissors, the bands released their hold and the package opened needs to stop' revealing disks from Empire Paper. It had to be the source of the smell in the lobby. The box reeked. She inserted the first recording.

> *'Empire, how may I direct your call?'*
> A strong man's voice rattled in response.
> *'Direct this to Empire's President, okay,'*
> Then he sang in monotone,
> *'Rock-abye baby on the tree top'*
> *'Cutting down trees now has to stop'*

Next he reverted to speech which wasn't very different.
'Somebody is going to pay'
Then the click and that was it.

David entered then with a tall gentleman from the police.

"Violet, this is Lieutenant James who is interested in the Empire case."

"Great, I've heard of your famous David informed me of the package just delivered from Empire. We're interested in the caller you just listened to. I headsolvings, Lieutenant. I'm pleased you're on the case."

"Thanks, Miss Easton. David informed me of the Empire package just delivered. We're interested in the caller you just listened to. I heard some outside the door.. At noon precisely, an explosion occurred at Empire Paper Mill, killing four workers. The tapes may offer clues. May I hear them?"

"Absolutely. The guy is a crazed tree hugger or something worse." She rewound everything and played it. Lieutenant James listened intently, then commented,

"What is there to compare to for identification of this psychopath?"

"I have enough recordings from Empire but I haven't had opportunity to compare yet. He could be anybody right now, even an employee or nobody remotely connected."

"Keep at it, Miss Easton, please. We need something to go on now. Again I appreciate your help"

"Sure thing. Call me Violet, though."

"Is there indication where that first call came from, Violet?"

"The tracer came up empty on the telephone number. Must have used a burn telephone or something else. I picked up a strange sound on the tape though – hydraulic air or whooshing sound. My ears matched it to city bus door opening. I'll play that back."

She did so and immediately James agreed it sounded like bus door opening at a stop.

"The bus station in Queens has an old-fashioned working pay phone that he could have used but that could be traced. If the guy had a burn phone and tossed it, what did he use for the next phone call. It's something else. There's a thing debt collectors use that gives false numbers to Caller ID display, often using your work number or a relative's phone so you'll pick up and answer it. That could be what he used. The device is illegal, but still it's used."

" Let's listen to the next phone call." Violet hurried on.

Violet felt increasing pressure for finding clues although that wasn't helping the nitty-gritty moving on. On the next tape from Empire was the same rattly voice, threatening, "A bomb is effective" and "This isn't going to stop. Tell Lieutenant James to find a way to keep disaster from happening at Staples, too. There's nothing the great detective can't do."

James stopped in the doorway and turned.

"That's always a bad sign when they get personal -thinking they're above the law, first then confident they can outwit everyone. I'm not great, but he envisions that to increase his desire for besting me. The challenge is out there. I have to accept it. I'll need copies of the tape recordings, Violet."

She immediately copied everything to a flash drive and handed them to him.

"Doesn't it disturb you that he is singling you out from other police in general?"

"Psychopaths often enjoy leading investigative detectives on a false trail taunting. It's nothing new to me."

The Golden State Killer, originally 'Nightstalker', delighted in using false red herrings for confusing police. I think we have to treat this as an implied bomb threat. Serial killers, the Zodiac Killer, not only threatened a bomb but included a 'recipe' for explosives in his communications. A sign they eventually want to be stopped though not usually consciously. I will do my best to stop it."

Tom walked in carrying a hand held. James was finishing up a call himself, "Yes, every Staples store – full protection, pronto." Though he felt like it was a line from an old movie, he said it anyway – "Be on the lookout for any suspicious characters," then he turned of the phone.

"Is that a phone call?" he asked Tom. "Who is calling and do I know you?"

"It's a company phone. My name's Tom Trumble. I don't know who's calling but he asked for you particularly. It's on speakerphone." James spoke one word into the phone, "James,"

"James"

"I heard your earlier question. Your Cadillac is easy to spot. There's only one business in the building, Angel Sound Technologies, for visiting. You should watch the news. Someone close to you is a major stockholder and therefore on my unlike list." The phone cut off.

Violet, who had been recording the conversation exchange switched on the television mounted above her own desk.

"Four Empire employees were killed today after an explosion in the pulp machine. The powerful explosive used is thought to be an IED initially implanted in the wood chipper. Details on six o'clock news."

"This is unfortunate. I've got to run now, a Staples store employee is reporting a break-in. Keep looking, Violet. It's imperative we find this guy before everything escalates."

CHAPTER SEVEN

Kelly Jo sighed at the no paper feed light blinking on the printer. Predictably, nobody brought in a new carton for refilling it. She found none in the storage closet and moaned that a trip to the loading dock was necessary now. Remembering that a delivery was just made eased her frustration. Passing the employee's bathroom, the smell of bleach wrinkled her nose. Kelly always had extreme sensitivity to that smell.

Noticing the girl outside cleaning she asked, "Is that chlorine I smell?"

The flustered employee responded, "I always use bleach – gets a good clean."

Kelly responded, "That's true" and moved on. She opened the door into the loading dock and found her nose assaulted. To her it was strong – the smell of human bathrooms – unflushed urine. She spoke immediately into the phone.

"Security is needed NOW on the loading dock." She explained the smell and though security first questioned it, they showed up. First guy in said, "It's probably cats. They roam free in the alley."

"No cat did this." she retorted. "It's human urine. I know it."

The second officer opened up a carton of paper. There it was – telltale yellow snits and the offensive odor. This guy knew of

Kelly's proclivity in identifying smells because he'd once asked her if the lunch he'd left in the refrigerator was still okay to eat. It wasn't.

They began searching every box and the chief of the company immediately called the police. They showed up with Lieutenant James arriving first. The lab van followed next.

"When did you expect the delivery?" he asked. By then management was involved and that branch manager spoke right up.

"We don't usually monitor deliveries. They show up when it's convenient to them."

"Where is the delivery sign-in sheet?"

"On the podium next to the dock door."

James checked for yesterday's entries and for that 'Abundant Paper' delivered eight cartons at 8:25 p.m.

"Did this company complain or have issues with Staple's operation – unpaid invoice or disrupted deliveries?"

"No, absolutely not. We've got a standing order, they're reliable and never had this problem before." the Office Manager responded. James processed the information and said, "Approximately how, long did this delivery sit unattended?"

"Overnight definitely, but the dock doors are locked at midnight when the security guard completes rounds."

"I'd like to speak with the guard to see if he noticed the smell then."

"Our security officer is a she, Corrine Franks. I'll page her. Her shift is starting."

Franks noticed no smell or unusual activity from last night.

"So the contaminant was introduced from 8:25 p.m. to midnight when security entered. Did anyone check employees who helped in unloading?"

"There was only one temp employee. He was only contracted for yesterday. He's long gone now."

"I'll need his contact information," James stated.

"Okay Lieutenant," the manager checked it on phone entries. "I'll try the agency since we don't have that information." A short conversation with the temp office led to a frown on the manager's wrinkled face. But he remained o9n the phone, telling James that the temp they sent never reported back.

"Get his license number. They must have it."

"Okay. It's Hb3799. "James sprinted out the dock onto the street's sidewalk and began searching cars parked in the area. He found the plate and the card had someone inside, not moving.

"Hynicki, get over here fast. Bring medical tech van too. Here's is my location now."

Hynicki responded and in twelve minutes they had revived the guy, thankfully not dead. Med Tech found an injection site and i8mmeditely administered sodium and glucose.

"This has to be the intended temp employee which the perpetrator got of the way. We're not going to find him with no trail to the temp office. Hynicki, see if you can find out anything useful from this guy here. We'll talk at headquarters after it."

Back inside the manager moaned, "I don't understand it. We've used that agency before and never had any trouble or impostors."

"Well, that's our guy, I'm convinced of that. Ruined boxes of paper is not fatal to anyone. I suggest you contact Abundance then move on. We'll impound the paper evidence, you'll get issued corporate credit, and the lab is working on identifying DNA from the urine. It won't exactly point to the culprit but will eventually aid in conviction later on. Thanks for your cooperation."

The lab found it was indeed human urine, confirming Kelley's sense of smell. James got in the Cadillac and drove to Bitsy's.

CHAPTER EIGHT

Wealthy widow Bitsy Schwartz, James' significant other, took the New York Times having it delivered in the lobby of her building. In the condo elevator, Eli stepped over the crack between floors and didn't see the paper lying in the usual spot and proceeded upstairs where Bitsy stood outside the elevator door.

"Welcome Eli, it's so pleasurable that you're here."

"Hi, Bitsy. I see you've retrieved today's paper. Any news about the opera murder?"

"I haven't even opened the paper yet. Sophia talked on the phone very long, most of that complaining. Understandably she was quite upset about what happened, especially why. Edward and Sophia f changed their seating and though she didn't accuse me for offering homeless tickets in the past, it was in her voice."

"I'm sorry Bitsy. Changing seats is her way of distancing the incident. It's understandable."

"Oh absolutely dear."

James held the inner door, gaining them entry into the opulent living room. Bitsy waited for James to settle in the chair usually preferred then set the newspaper next to him and sat herself.

"It won't be in the paper yet, though you should know there was an explosion at Empire."

"Oh dear, you know I have investments/ stockholding in Empire."

"That's part of the reason I'm here now – after just enjoying your company. There was an implied threat to you. I wanted the assurance that everything's okay."

"I'm fine. Are you sure there's nothing about it in the paper? They're fairly fast reporting things."

She reached over, unfolding its front page. Immediately a snakeskin dropped out onto Eli's outstretched leg. He jumped up uttering a few choice words he needed to apologize to Bitsy for.

She brushed it away, "It's okay, just the skin off a rattler – nothing inside."

"Bitsy, you never fail in amazing. How did you know it's a rattlesnake?"

"Believe it or not, Eli, I was a girl scout. I remember the description from camping experiences. The question is how did it get there in the newspaper?"

James responded, "George delivers that newspaper at four o'clock>"

"Yes, Nolan my former husband, liked reading the evening edition sitting at the bar with a neat whiskey. Roxie receives it now. You know Roxie, right?"

"I certainly do. Seems like the name Dolores would fit better though."

"One can hardly rename employees when physical appearance does not match them. Anyway, Roxie opens the outer door for George at four o'clock. If she';s taking a call, or you know, using the facilities, she leaves that open."

"Right there, Bitsy, that's got to stop immediately! - leaving the door open even briefly. We might be facing a maniac capable of killing because of loose connections in his mind. He probably would not hesitate to take Roxie out for gaining access to you."

"ELI," Bitsy stood hands on hips, "Where did this machismo come from? I appreciate your concern however I know the strengths of the staff and my inner resources. I'm quite capable. You might think Roxie's thick in the middle, but no, she carries a gun and wouldn't hesitate to use it if necessary."

James' protective instinct remained strong, though this was as close to fighting as he ever wanted to get. The condo security served efficiently, Roxie wasn't negligent and Bitsy showed up spunky as per usual.

"It's just that I've been involved in two rattlesnake troubles today.. I'm not obsessive about it but somebody's trying to scare us using snakes and I don't like it. Angel Sound Technology is working to get a handle on this murderer. He is going to be caught."

"I'm sure that is true, with you on the job."

"in the meantime, Bitsy, be very careful, increase security measures and tell me of anything unusual."

"You know I will. Take care of yourself too. This guy knows you by name, even the Cadillac Seville you usually drive. Maybe you might change cars. The Bentley is available."

"I can picture that as attracting undue attention, though."

"Where re you going next?"

"I'm taking this snakeskin over to the lab then calling on Empire. I'll be back, then we can eat. Should I stop at Robert Allan's to get takeout?"

"That'd be great. I put the skin in a baggie – here."

"Thanks veery much dear. Lock up after I leave.'

"Be sure I will."

James kissed Bitsy on the cheek and went to the elevator.

Before going to the lab, he stopped in at Empire to check on progress. The bomb squad had not left yet and he asked about their findings. Zach Sommers was in charge. James asked, "What is the preliminary finding?"

"Nothing preliminary about it," answered Zach, exhibiting a powerful presence. "Whoever did it used a blasting cap to ignite fertilizer – urea nitrate."

"Wasn't that used at the World Trade Center bombing,?" James recalled.

"You know about that?"

"Yes, not your usual bomb explosive," James replied adding, "1993 that's how it happened. Chemical formula for that is $CH_5N_3O_4$. It is soluble and common in improvised bombs in Pakistan, Afghanistan, and now Iraq."

"I guess for a policeman, you're more knowledgeable than I thought." James ignored the left-handed compliment as Zach continued, "It's easily attainable and very effective, too."

"Thanks Zach, anything else important?"

"I'll let you know, Lieutenant."

James stopped in the office for the names of the murdered employees. Bitsy would want to express condolences personally to the families.

James next went to the couple's go to restaurant where owner, Robert Allan, greeted him. "Lieutenant James, it is always a pleasure."

"Robert, call me Eli. I like being here too. Bitsy sends her greeting."

"She's a fine lady you're lucky to have."

"Don't I know it every day."

"What are you thinking of tonight?"chef specialties are you thinking of tonight?"

"Bitsy's favorite is Chrunchy Vegetable Cakes. You should know what mine is since I order that regularly."

"Oh course, NY Steak with garlic cream, no potato, cheese grits instead, right?"

"Yes, it's always delicious. Thanks."

James waited for his food order which came in 15 minutes, told Robert goodnight then hurried back over to Bitsy's.

The Rattler, Jake, returned from the pet store and deposited the dead mice in the refrigerator. He wasn't planning on being gone very long but didn't want smelling rodents in the cage while he was looking at the World Wildlife Site on the screen, he found an interesting tidbit:

"Each year the Amazon loses fo9rested areas the size of the state of Delaware, usually from illegal logging." He thought that significant enough to travel there to stop it and he booked the flight to Peru.

"How would you venomous reptiles like visiting the Amazon Rainforest? Meet up with mambas, coral snakes or boa constrictors? No, I'd have to go through security or get special permission. Sorry, guys." He picked up a Bowie knife and slashed the snakes until they no longer moved and emptied the remains in the trash. The next day, he dumped the trash and muttered,

"I can't allow being tracked now. My work's important."

Grabbing a suitcase, he packed enough for a week, then closed it up and headed to the highway on Interstate 72. Driving his old Toyota, Jake pulled into the fast lane. A tree trimming truck blocked the right lane of the highway. He pulled over and stopped in front of it. Jumping out of the car, he released the truck's parking brake and quickly returned to the Toyota. As he took off down the highway, he saw the workers in the rear mirror, running after their truck and the cutter in the overhead bucket fall out. He was glad for it and the fact that he was using a stolen license plate in case they made note of it.;

CHAPTER NINE

Jake parked the Toyota, with another changed plate, in the long-term lot in airport parking. Getting his boarding pass from the kiosk with no checked baggage, he moved toward the gate. The seven hour flight to Peru was uneventful. On landing in Jose Chavez International Airport, he bought tickets for Iquitos, deep in the Amazon Rainforest and his planned encounter with the drug cartel. They would lead him to areas of deforestation where they often planted coca.

The coca plant thrives best in hot damp and humid locations such as the clearings of forests. The cartel got advanced knowledge of deforestation, going at night for planting coca. Somebody in the organization must use movements of tree killers to find areas they'll eradicate next. . It was time for

Walking in the airport, he found, among several excursion companies, Amazing Amazon Outings. Using cash he purchased a five day tour. It didn't matter since he planned on leaving it to find the tree killers. Then he visited the marketplace outside for needed supplies – extra light clothing, a backpack, cans of insect repellent and a machete. The outings company inside had them too, only much higher in price. He also found the market that had urea nitrate and fireworks too. He got both including a can of kerosene, tucking them in clothing in the large backpack. It was time for the excursion bus to take him to the launch for the river so he hurried there for the bus. Finding a window seat, he ignored the view of Iqitos Open Market, intensely studying the maps Amazing Amazon Outings provided free. The group was headed to Tahago Lodge, sort of a bare bones accommodation close to Tamshiyacu Reserve first destination. Information looked at in a pamphlet said the lodge had enough amenities and not as bare bones as he thought. He examined the aerial ma, determining it to be twenty miles from the river launch.

The bus was nearing the launch site. He folded the maps, grabbed his gear, and got off without talking to anyone, though several people talked around him. He wasn't interested but knew he'd have to later on if they spoke directly to him. It didn't happen and he remained aloof essentially unapproachable until boarding the launch riverboat. There were extravagant riverboats that had accommodations, jacuzzis, meals and nightlife that cruised the Amazon in Peru. This was not one of those. A wooden skull housed eight long benches, seating four people on each. Attached to flimsy metal poles on the port and starboard sides was a vinyl cloth roof to diminish, not necessarily eliminate the sun's intense effect. Jake reminded himself he picked this outing's lack of luxury for saving money. It was only for twenty miles anyway. Jake pushed forward, bumping people to move up in line. He wasn't fluent, but he thought he heard someone swear near him as his bag jostled one passenger.

"Cuidado! Senor."

"Pare."

Jake recognized Spanish for stop and did it. The captain of the vessel had spoken it and Jake would be foolish to ignore that if he wanted to board with no trouble. Turning full face to the captain, Jake used the international sign for movie, rotating his right hand around and over while cupping his eye like using a lens. The captain, Gregory, immediately smiled and directed Jake to the stern near the pilot's seat. Jake suspected he'd have to keep up the facade of filmmaker if he sat there, flicked the fleas on his phone and said the best his high school Spanish could offer.

"La luz. Mas mejor aqui." He pointed to a window seat far in the back of the boat. Captain Gregory frowned at first, imagining he would be featured in an upcoming movie. Jake picked up on that and took numerous photos of him from the stern. It seemed to appease him and he started the journey down the Amazon using his best tour guiding speech.

As foreign sounds of strange fauna reached his ears over Captain Gregory's booming voice, Jake shifted attention to the floral wonders and trees on the shore of the great Amazon River. He definitely noticed the spectacular natural elements all around him. Giant water lilies flourished nearby and hummingbirds landing on Monkey Bush flowers, Passion flowers or orchids enhanced the scenery. He reached into the backpack, taking out The Berkeley Guide to the Amazon Rainforest to see if that tree on starboard side was identified. It had wood vines up the trunk. Reading through the guide he saw one like it pictured. The name of it was Liana. It actually was the woody vine that climbed up another tree that he recognized as an Ironwood Tree. Macaws lived in it and its nesting site for Harpy Eagles, the world's very powerful birds of prey. Hoping to see one, he watched eagerly, through the camera's photo function (in case the Captain was looking over his way). The Ironwood tree could live seven hundred years though it's threatened by deforestation. He looked up ahead and saw a rubber tree, unexpectantly small in size. The guide credited its proliferation to the 1880's boom in rubber in the United States. He noted the Mahogany Tree was among trees labeled vulnerable. 50% of mahogany production was from illegal logging operations. Consumer demand fueled that. His anger rose as the vessel passed it and the Huimba Tree, which the Tacoma Indians believed held evil spirits in the trunk and cutting it down unleashed the evil to mankind.

Jake believed that cutting down any tree brought undue harm. His tall Birch in childhood was the epitome of perfect. Great climbing branches, a tree house on second rung was his entire world then. ...Until that day....he didn't want to remember it, but the memory – that fateful day he ran to the tree, his haven.... There were branches scattered everywhere and the tree-house in splinters. Pipes for a new sewage access were lined up where the beautiful shade had once been. He felt the disappointment and anger afresh.

Jake couldn't afford getting distracted now though. The riverboat was nearing the lodge embankment. He took one last look at the trees around him, vowing to protect them whatever it took.

Nearest to shore were the tallest of trees forming a canopy upward. The Wemba, useful Lupuna, which was probably used in filling the sleeping bag he got at the market grew there. Strangler figs and ficus grew unchecked close to shore, their buttressed root systems in soil on the moist riverbank. He checked the guide to identify the magnificent Brazil Nut Tree. He read of the delicate ecotourism involved in its survival. Pollination from the indigenous Euglosia Bee was necessary and the bee required the scent of a certain orchid to attract important female bees. Cycle of life evident here. No wasted creatures or creations. For a moment Jake felt something akin to spiritual. It didn't last very long. The boat, fast approaching shore now, was scraping on the shallowq river bottom.

The lodge fee was paid earlier in the package price arranged in the airport so he only needed the room key. He told the clerk that he was too involved in filming to go on the scheduled tour tomorrow but that his room didn't need cleaning. She only laughed, "We don't even have a housekeeping staff this week. There are sheets and towels in that alcove over there if needed."

"Thank you. Gracias," Jake replied and left with the key in hand. The room was only adequate but that didn't matter. He half-reclined on the bed and read the brochure the overly friendly guy on the launch gave him. It was surprising to learn it wasn't all logging operations triggering most deforestation, but agricultural farming too. It was worth remembering. It didn't change his mind about interrupting loggers though. It only gave him more incentive to harm the people exploiting and removing trees. Those hell bent on destroying them needed punished.

Jake inventoried the supplies he brought. It was all good. Bags of snacks, dried fruit, banana chips, and nutritious protein bars, went in his backpack. He viewed the photos taken of the tall trees and of course, the captain, then slept for tomorrow's excursion to the jungle.

CHAPTER TEN

The sound of rain on the lodge roof woke him up and he glanced at his watch. 5 a.m., time to get going. Not needing to go to the lobby for anything, he grabbed his gear and exited through the closest door. Pulling his hood up he set off through the underbrush marking the trail to the interior of the rainforest. Though humid, the temperature wasn't oppressive. Various bird calls had him looking up to the tree tops where spectacled owls, macaws, and unusual parrots were perched. He had no time for that and pressed on. His ear became accustomed to the jungle sound of birds and tropical animals. He listened intently to hear human voices nearby though. At one point he rested and took out food he'd purchased earlier. Stashing the wrappers in his backpack, he rejoined the thick foliage and cacophony of the environment. About one mile further into the rainforest, he heard familiar chopping sounds. Someone was up ahead destroying trees. Not knowing if he was going to find farmers or loggers, maybe even drug cartel, he took out the machete and the important item he'd had to declare in checked baggage, A Smith-Wesson Model 686 semi-automatic revolver.

There in the clearing up ahead was a native woman hewing a Liana tree with only a hand held ax. He put the weapon in the back then yelled over, "Hey stop that, Hey, Paro eso, he said in Spanish. The woman looked up, stopped using the ax, dropped it and ran off into the rainforest, leaving the coca plants intended for the soil. Jake examined and picked up a few and kept them in a zippered bag for later. He headed further into the rainforest. He wasn't going to bother over the woman who was not a primary player in tree deforestation. Those major despicables were up ahead and he pressed on.

Now the sun's heat beat down from it's higher position in the sky. The jungle awakened in active response. It was hot. Using the machete, Jake forged a path for the next five miles through the surrounding thickness. A spectacled owl hoot faded into the sound of chopping trees and he knew the logging operation was nearby. He had the ingredients for a bomb in the backpack and shifted the weight of that on the shoulders. He'd have to gain the trust of the workers to get close enough to set it up. He took a bottle of whiskey from his gear and opened it, took a swig, though it wasn't something he preferred, and entered the cleared area. Two native men were chopping down rubber trees using a large machine , powerful enough for devouring wood. They looked up at him. He held up the bottle, approaching them with a smile. They halted and grabbed their guns. In confidence Jake proceeded and spoke in Spanish equivalent of "I hope work's made you thirsty. It's hot out today. Can I help?"

The men seemed to accept it and showed him the branches waiting for the wood chopper. They watched him at first, then took turns at the refreshment. After a bit, they fell asleep. Jake set up the nitrate bomb and detonated it and took off fast. He heard voices in the clearing and knew other workers were arriving to destroy more of the trees. If they approached the bomb, they'd be blown up too. He raced to escape for his own safety, secure in the belief that those lives lost were collateral damage. Following his previous trail, he reached the path that led back into the lodge.

The radio station in Lima, 102.1, reported the explosion in the rainforest. Jake heard that in the lobby while he picked up food to eat later.

"An explosion of unknown origin resulted in several deaths and extensive damage to logging equipment. The unfortunate victims had been drinking whiskey and it is thought they abandoned those while a dissident opposed to deforestation destroyed their access to it. Police have no leads to his identity. Stay tuned for developments on this station in Lima."

Jake ignored the deaths again only being necessary and returned to his room, pre-checking out, for needed sleep. He had enough big plans for returning to New York tomorrow and ate enough for satisfying body tonight and lay down feeling fulfilled. 'Trees are safe, I'm okay, that's good"

Keeping the radio frequency on, the next news concerned Peru's soccer victory over Mexico. Jake smiled at that as in his boyhood he'd played soccer once enjoying it. He took the tree guide, four remaining blasting caps and tucked there safely in planned checked baggage.

CHAPTER ELEVEN

Back in New York, he couldn't escape the news highlighting the hoarding of toilet paper. Frenzied people were stocking up in epic buying sprees to obtain it. In Peru, especially Cuzco, gateway to Macchu Pichu ruins, paper was not used. It clogged sewage systems. Tourists had to adapt.

Toilet paper is responsible for uprooting 27,000 trees a day from the rainforest. Jake remember that Americans use 36.5 billion rolls every year from the result of pulping 15 million trees. "Lots of trees uselessly destroyed," he thought.

He returned to his home, cognizant of the radio now calling him The Rattler from previous murders, and was surprised to find a letter in his door, addressed to Jake Arnold Glaxton, not The Rattler.

He set that inside and checked the bonsai. Though they didn't need much water, he spritzed each anyway. Opening the mail, an official letter from the credit card company needed attention.

"Dear Mr. Glaxton, While we pride ourselves on the secure service we offer, we regret to inform you of a security breach. An unauthorized agent has hacked the information in your file, revealing name, address and credit card number. What you need to do is contact a lawyer. We will pay for expenses. The agent handling this is John Smythe. He will endeavor to assist you with his expertise in security breaches. Using him is gratis and part of the concern for customers we value. Thank you.

Jake's initial response was to leave immediately – typical adrenaline response of flight or fight, only he decided on fight. He'd seen it in movies, James Bond type of villain who even invited police in, being very clever, essentially tainting investigators. "Come and get me now, if you can."

Among the names or of companies that were possible recipients of his personal information he saw one surprise, "Angel Sound Technology". That was where Jake had found Lieutenant James once. He checked on the computer and that company was also investigating the homeless man he blew up at the opera. So they knew his address, even his name. There was nothing here to tie him to the murder of Theodore Barnes or the homeless person. They couldn't know how he knew and hated him or why. He never used paper so the only loose trail was in the computer or the phone. He took the time to erase files and highlight preserving of trees in business files. Satisfied there weren't any threads for implicating him, he fixed lunch and enjoyed eating.

The Rattler then read about toilet paper use. The hoarding of it was big news. Not surprising, toilet paper's responsible for uprooting 27,00 trees a day. It included hardwoods and other varieties. $ ply thick is from virgin pulp which Americans use 36.5 billion rolls every year, resulting in pulping of 15 million trees. He shook his head and tensed for what he had to do.

CHAPTER TWELVE

Lieutenant James looked up from the report of last night to the uniformed man standing there.

"What is it officer? He asked.

"They told me to notify you, sir. A body was found outside of Georgia Pacific's warehouse, "the dutiful officer responded. "What's odd is it's a rattlesnake bite."

"How do you know that's it?"

"Well my partner is an experienced camper. He recognized it immediately."

"What's his name?"

"Toby Gray, sir."

"Thank you, Simmonds," James replied reading the officer's name tag. "Hang here a minute if you will."

James called in Joe Hynicki from the squad room next to his office. Hynicki was a valued friend and colleague from a blowfish poisoning case in Manhattan. Tall as James, Hynicki appeared in the doorway.

"Great! Joe, I've got something for your skills of investigation now. Have you seen Officer's Simmonds report on the Georgia Pacific murder?"

"Yes sir. It just came up. What's needed?" Joe responded.

"Two things. On a previous murder at the opera, we don't have the victim's name. He frequented Light of Hope Mission and hung out near there. Anything you can find about his identity is good and helpful in finding why he was killed and more importantly who did it."

"On it. What next?"

"As you know, a rattlesnake killed our current dead body. Unless there is a rogue snake roaming around on our city streets – all officers laughed – someone had to purchase it, transport it to the warehouse, then retrieve it after the murder. Ask around in the neighborhoods nearby to see if anyone noticed anything unusual."

"Yes, Sir."

"I doubt you'll find witnesses especially at that hour and it's not residential only industrial. I think The Rattler counted on that."

"I do that right away then investigate the homeless place. Anything further, Lieutenant?"

"No that's good enough. Thanks Hynicki." James turned toward Simmonds asking,

"Is your car available?"

"It's ready and waiting."

"Let's go now. Can't have a dead body lying out on the street when everyone gets to work."

Climbing into the squad car, James asked the officer driving, "You Toby?"

"Yes, sir. It's about ten blocks away. We'll be there in no time."

Pulling up to the curb, James hopped out. He removed the tarp covering the body and inspected the wound.

"It's definitely a rattlesnake bite, only unlike the Barnes victim, it's on the neck. How could that even happen?"

Toby answered. "The worker was unloading boxes of toilet paper. One box is partly open. Perp must have hidden the snake inside it and when he shouldered it picking up he got bitten."

"All for toilet paper…", James muttered out loud.

"Speaking of which, there was urea fertilizer in several boxes," Gray added.

"He was planning on blowing them only got interrupted," James guessed.

"What kind of fool plans to blow up toilet paper?"

"Only a crazy one. Obviously we're not dealing with a very rational person." James continued, "Any fingerprints found?"

"No nothing."

Hynicki approached in his car and parked it, got out and walked to them.

"Lieutenant, no witnesses found to the crime, however a watchman on rounds spotted an old Toyota parked near the plant entrance. His rounds were an hour apart and the car wasn't there later on."

"Did he observe the plate number?" James asked.

"Said it was facing in the opposite direction, so no."

"Damn, that would have been nice"

"Maybe there is this help. On the front bumper was a sticker for the Amazon Rainforest"

"Interesting, before I left for here, Interpol reported an explosion in the rainforest in Peru- two killed using urea nitrate fertilizer bomb. We need to track travelers there recently. Maybe we'll get a name. Also research who bought a new rattler. The other one is surely dead."

Hynicki yelled a "yes, sir" as he hurried to his car to get on it.

CHAPTER THIRTEEN

It's ten o'clock and Violet's working in Angel Sound Technology this morning. Robin is home for today. Violet wanted to listen to the old tape recording of the bonsai salesman later though Robin had hidden it well. She glanced at the bonsai near her desk. Tiny white insects were dominating the moistness inside. She needed to do something immediately. Checking online she called the expert on bonsais.

The response after entering the number was, "Healthy Bonsai Helpline. What do you need?"

"In the soil around the bonsai trees, is infestation of tiny white bugs. I'm afraid they're destroying the tree," she answered.

The deep rattly voiced responded,"Is the soil moist now?"

Violet touched it and affirmed it, "Yes."

"Are they wingless insects or capable of flying?"

"I think wingless."

"It's probably springtails. If you've got cinnamon nearby, apply it to soil now, and twice weekly for two weeks using chopstick technique in soapy water. If the surface is a blanket of white something stronger's needed. Is it?"

"Oh yes definitely. I can barely see the soil through the insects."

"Do you have a Walmart Supercenter or Staples nearby?"

Violet paused when the man's voice uttered "Staples". Something in the back of her mind triggered recognition of that voice. 'I've heard it before,' she thought, 'only where?' The Staples threatener on the phone was the only time that word and sound came together. She took a risk _ "What's your name?" she asked the caller.

"Jake"

"Something about your voice is familiar to me. I've heard it before."

Jake sensed it was getting dangerous to continue talking. Though he liked talking to this girl, the possibility of traced calls, giving financial information, or just this Angel Sound Technology woman's remembering that he had telephoned before, felt very threatening to him, but he needed her name to make sure it was her when he did what he planned to do to her to prevent her from disclosing his identity to anyone.

"What's your name, honey?"

"Violet Easton"

"Get yourself some neem oil for disinfecting the bonsai at Walmart. There's no charge for today." He hung up immediately.

Though the man upset her, his advice was probably good for the bonsai. Violet set down the cellphone on the table near the door and looked for the coat she wore into work.

"That's right. I left that on a hanger in the break room. When she left to get it, Tom picked up her cellphone and entered his number and retrieved the password for the Find My Phone function. Sneaky or shameful, he didn't care as he did care about Violet. He'd become enamored with her passionate enthusiastic soul, though knowing it could result in harm if someone took advantage of her.

CHAPTER FOURTEEN

Violet awoke feeling weak and disoriented. Sacks of flour and bags of sugar everywhere filled up the space in the room. She took mental inventory, trying to remember what had happened earlier to explain her presence here. Though her head hurt, she pushed past it to the feeling of a knife to her back, then the man forcing her into his car. The image got clearer and riding in an old Toyota popped up. A pinprick in her arm was as far as she could remember – the mental vision going to blank screen. She lay on her side on the uncomfortable mattress tossed on the floor.

"Who is this guy?" she thought. "Why is he targeting me?" She didn't know his full name now, although he had to be the bonsai expert, Jake from the phone – the assault in Walmart's parking lot implied he knew she was going there following his instruction. Her head hurt but thoughts got through like the one when she thought of him on the phone. His voice matched the caller threatening Empire Paper Mill earlier. She knew her voice recognition ability was right.

In her mind, the word "phone" opened up other channels simultaneously with her emotional balance registering danger. 'This guy is intent on murder – has done it before.' It started her fear/flight function going full force. She tried to think rationally – 'Had she noted anything helpful on the way here?'

The adrenaline response was very strong and interfered with her usual balanced thoughts. "What weapon could be used?"

First, she came up with nothing, then found her purse next to the mattress. "Of course, the phone!"

She grabbed the handle of the purse and searched inside it. Getting frantic wouldn't help. Being very careful she explored the inner contents. No phone or anything useful as a weapon either. No pepper spray or something sharp.

Now despair joined the emotion of fear. The mind is amazing, though, when it's under pressure. An image appeared of a neighborhood store. Remembering she saw it just before the car stopped. It was Rosita's Bakery. It had to be nearby. If only she could use the phone, informing her location would help police or someone else find her in time. Laying her aching head on the pillowless mattress underneath her, she succumbed to feeling groggy and doomed to fate.

A comforting feeling came to her when a favorite childhood song played in her head.

> *Sing on the way to heaven*
> *Angel voices show the way*
> *It's a pleasing sound in God's ear*
> *Move on, rejoicing with no fear*
>
> *Make a joyful noise*
> *Like a choir of girls and boys*
> *Heavin is near – no need to steer*
> *Follow the angel voices*

As she sang it, one peculiar sound permeated the room. She listened intently. IT WAS A RATTLE!

Her acuity for discerning sound heightened. Fear intensified when in between rattles, slithering on the floor confirmed the presence of a snake close by. She drew her legs up into her chest in reaction. Not that it mattered even. A rattlesnake might strike anywhere on the body not only exposed limbs. In impossible situations, Violet found strength in faith and singing. Her voice quivered at first singing *Amazing Grace* but strengthened on the third verse. Listening intermittently for snake sounds, there were none after singing. Was it ridiculous to imagine the snake heard the soothing voice and quit moving forward toward her now?

Scanning the room, the viper was nowhere near the mattress. Good sign. Being very careful, Violet tiptoed to the door which was, of course, locked outside. Though she didn't have *ophidiophobia* (fear of snakes) she did not want to die from one. On the way back, her eyes traced movement in the back of the room. Focusing and walking very fast, she saw it was curled up sedate though unwinding slowly, slithering with no rattling. She remembered reading once that herpavores hear using vibrations. There had to be some from walking on the floor. Reaching the bed she took one look at the room setup. No windows. There in the center of bags was a glass cage, presumably for the rattlesnake. She noted its location in relation to hers and where the snake was now. The cage had a lid near it that might lock it in. There wasn't time now for planning – the rattler was moving forward in the room now.

Violet prayed and commenced singing. The snake, quiet now, was on top of the glass enclosure though only the outside edge. Violet first considered rushing there and clamping on the lid if the snake went fully inside. Not probable though. She hesitated knowing it might take the opportunity to bite her as she tried it. Indecision meant loss of opportunity window but desperation usually needed taking a risk. She watched fixedly as the snake inched up the edge, then primed her muscles and mental energy to spring up. In that state of anticipation, she waited.

CHAPTER FIFTEEN

The noise of the room door hitting the inside wall sent her heart rate into orbit, but she kept fixing her eyes on the snake. Snake hearing was not good for human voices (200-300mgHz) though vibration was definitely heard. Simultaneously as a familiar man crashed into the room noisily, the rattler slithered down the enclosure and headed toward him.

"Tom, watch out! She shouted frantically. "The rattlesnake is headed your way."

Violet started singing *Home on the Range*, softly and rhythmically to calm the snake into reverse. It didn't work. Still singing in hopes it might, she looked over to Tom Trumble noting he was wearing lead gloves, thick boots and extra body protection. How did he know it was a snake?, she thought. In the outer room shadows, another man was visible wearing similar gear. Violet wanted to break into the Hallelujah Chorus now when recognizing Lieutenant James out there. Instead of singing, she got up and moved far away from her rescuers. They had on protection which she did not and if they succeeded in trapping the rattler, good. If they only scared the thing, it might head her way.

With a soft voice, James spoke first, "Violet don't move. Stay where you are now. Keep singing though. You're like an Indian snake charmer."

She sang in song, "Watch loud noise now. It thinks you're the enemy. Be very careful. Glad you're here. He is near the cage in center."

Violet stopped singing and the rattler moved forward toward the door. As the snake inched forward toward the men, James and Tom moved left away from the broken door opening. Violet was safely near the mattress on the other side. James feared the snake would block the exit and risked using the phone, calling Special Forces due there very soon.

"James, here. We're trapped inside the room with the rattler. Please hurry up. Any suggestions?"

Using a calm voice, Lionel O'hara said, "Hang on Lieutenant. Do nothing to startle it. We heard singing earlier. If everybody sings and it calms the viper, good. Stop if it agitates. Track it's location for us. We're just outside." James was feeling the tension,but still had humor.

"What do you suggest for a tune?"

"Oh – how about *Slithery Dee?*"

Continuing the open connection on the phone, James noted snake location and stared at the open door, as the suited men and one woman entered holding nets, needles full of sedatives and a dead mouse. James moved toward them and Tom walked quietly, carefully over toward Violet in the imprisoning room. No exchange between them happened though reassuring smiles and hope was evident in their eyes. James felt the duty and fascination of watching the experts dispatch the creature that had brought fearful feelings and overwhelming adrenaline rushes to the trio. The rattlesnake went for the mouse, injected with sedatives, and Sally placed it in the glass enclosure. She had trouble locking up the lid but O'Hara set it straight. By now the viper was falling asleep and no threat remained. Violet immediately hugged Tom and thanked Lieutenant James for the rescue.

"How did you find me?" she asked.

"Where is this guy who kidnapped me? Why? Is he still a threat?" "How did you know wearing snake protection was even needed?"

Violet's query was understandable, though the snake-handlers were removing the cage and James began singing,

> *"Oh the Slithery Dee*
> *he crawled out of the sea*
> *you may catch all the others*
> *but you won't catch me."*

The others joined in,
> *"You Evil Viper"* (Tom)
> *"Belly Scooter"* (Violet)
> *"Slick Fang Ground Dweller"* (James).

CHAPTER SIXTEEN

Jake had no intention of returning to the sleeping space in back of the bakery, he had rented for murdering the girl. He used false name and information, for paying rent, cash. He was upset for losing the rattler but once again, collateral damage. The rattler served its purpose for eliminating the girl. He'd read "The Girl Who Knew Too Much" This one knew the connection between his tree business and the Empire murders. She had to go, though if they met in other circumstances, he'd have even liked her.

The rattler's first bite might not kill her instantly, but with no food for it, it would repeatedly strike until she succumbed to the venom. Oh well. Right now he had to vacate his apartment and hole up somewhere. From online racetrack betting, he had enough money to go anywhere in the world. He followed his original plan, parked and began loading up the Toyota with a computer and other essentials, leaving nothing behind to indicate his identity. No room for the bonsai—he lined them up on the sidewalk for others to take. He had no paper, so using a sign like "Don't Overwater!" was not possible. Shrugging his shoulders in resignation, he drove off.

CHAPTER SEVENTEEN

Violet, Lieutenant James and Tom stood on the sidewalk taking in the beautiful sky and being grateful. Violet was still shaking inside, and needed the sit down.

"I need a beer guys. When I get back to the apartment, I'm gonna indulge!"

Tom immediately broke in, "Wait a nanosecond! You're staying at my place for now."

"Tom, I couldn't impose. What's wrong with my own apartment?"

"For one thing, this murdering menace now knows where that is. He had access to contents of your purse, including driver's license information—No, you're not going there."

James knew a conflict between a "macho man" and woman when he saw it, and so spoke up. "There's a Nurse Nancy's up there next to Rosita's Bakery—just the bar we need. Come on now, you two."

Only a block up, they went in and ordered a beer each. The waitress, wearing a flimsy white tank-top and a stethoscope, set down their order. "Miss Nancy at your service. Need anything else?" Of all the lines in James' mind that he could come back

MURDERS OF THE RATTLER

with now, most got censored by good judgment, so it came out, "Are you the bar owner, Nancy?"

"Oh Heaven, no! We all use the name 'Nancy' to keep customers from knowing the real ones. Obsessive patrons chasing isn't fun."

"I understand. I'm a policeman, now wondering if a man with a rattly voice came in in the last few days for drinks?"

"Hmm... 'rattly'..."

Violet provided the exact sound of her kidnapper's voice. "Go get neem oil at Walmart."

"Nancy" put a hand to her head, "Okay, I remember him – ordered a birch beer – only drank half hurriedly and left enough money on the table, gave me a tip from his wallet and was gone."Did he use a name?"

"No name but I found this on the floor. Returning to the register, she came back with a flyer.

"The Convention of Tree Cutters"

"It's tomorrow," James noted the date.

"Come view the big machines they use in the Rainforest," it read inside.

"Boy, that'll get this guy."

Information included "5 minutes out of city in a sleepy little town, Double Tree Inn. Directions included with $40 registration. Motel accommodation extra. 478-3511-1000." "Helpful info Nancy, thanks." Violet and Tom ordered another beer while James excused himself. "I'll be back. There's something I'm going to check at Rosita's Bakery.

"While you in there, how 'bout sweets for us?" Tom asked.

"What is your intended guilty pleasure?" James retorted.

"Elephant ears."

"Cinnamon rolls," Violet chimed in.

"Okay, I'll get those."

CHAPTER EIGHTEEN

At Rosita's, James tried to not drool looking inside the cases of sweets inside. Life-threatening encounters made him very hungry though. He waited as the clerk finished with another customer, then asked, "Are you the bakery owner?"

"Yes, that is me, Rosita."

"I'm a policeman—rank is Lieutenant actually."

Rosita gasped and said, "I do what's right, I pay taxes, nothing illegal here."

"No worries. I only need to know who rented the area in the back in the last few days."

"Oh I see. That was an informal transaction. Not rent exactly. I thought he was homeless and he had enough cash, $35. It's just a storage space with a mattress inside. Extra money type thing.

An American name he used with a rattling voice like a drinker often does – John Chapman. Am I in trouble now officer?" Rosita frowned , worrying.

"Not at all. There is an officer in the back now and the department will pay for other damages. We had to break down the door for rescue."

"Oh my God! Was that man injured?"

"No, he attempted to injure someone else instead. "You're not involved. It's police business; we'll keep you informed. Now, I'd like some of these lovely baked goods."

"Of course, Lieutenant. Which ones?"

"Four baklava, two cinnamon rolls, two elephant ears, and whatever a 'singing hinnie' is—three, maybe, of them. That's all."

"Singing hinnie is a gridle-fried honey cake with currant inside."

"Give me one to try," James requested. "I'll pay either way." James thought currant flavor would be like a usual berry taste. He bit into it. It was not even close. Swallowing carefully, he wrapped the remaining singing hinnie in a napkin from the counter and deposited it in his pocket. He paid for the order, tipping Rosita nicely, then took the bag out to the street. To banish the currant's foreign taste, he took out and ate a baklava square. Very delicious, and a favorite. Smiling, he returned to Nurse Nancy's and his companions. Opening the sack, James handed an elephant ear to Tom as they were on top. Since the cinnamon rolls were further down, he explained to Violet that the singing hinnies were for her.

"I've heard of these—thanks! Anything connected to singing has to be good." She took a bite and grinned. "It's delicious! I love currants."

No comment on that from Lieutenant James—he face puckered. "I spoke to Rosita about the person using the back room. She thought the guy was homeless—named 'John Chapman.' Ring any bells?"

Tom was first to answer. "That's Johnny Appleseed's real name, if I recall."

"Right. But… that is no help in finding a murderer. I'm going to invoke my best Paul Bunyan imitation to attend the convention of the cutters. It's quite probable this nasty 'Rattler' will disrupt and interfere there. While I was gone, what did you decide on for sleeping arrangement tonight?"

James usually avoided prying into situations involving personal relationships, but it was important to know where Violet was for police protection and to tap into her knowledge of the murderer's voice.

"I'm staying with Tom," Violet said softly.

Though those two had worked it out earlier, Tom said for James' benefit, "I have an extra bedroom not used and security in my building is excellent."

"That's good," James replied. "There will be an officer on duty there until the threat to her is over."

James savored another baklava and motioned to "Miss Nancy" they were heading out. She collected the tab and responded to their thanks in kind. James hesitated then held up the flyer Nancy had found.

"Thanks for this especially. You might have helped us in catching a murderer."

"Well I hope that's true. Nobody should get away with that" – she hesitated – "Oh maybe this will help too. The guy paid in cash but when he opened his wallet I stared inside. I'm far-sighted you see. There was one card sticking out and there was a name – It was Glaxton." James almost did a foot dance, but only said, "Okay, thanks."

CHAPTER NINETEEN

In a motel room, reruns of television show Gold Rush played on as Karl slept. He only watched for the powerful machines, not the story. Though he had noticed Parker, the featured actor was very young, in late teens in this version. Karl's eyes opened to the convention poster over the desk. There his old mug face stared back. It was a professionally done enough photo. 'Not so bad', he thought.

> *"Featured is Karl, 'Atlas' Gruber relating tales of logging the Amazon Rainforest and stories of the big machines you'll see on the convention floor."*

Karl checked the time – six hours until his speech- then opened the styrofoam container full of ribs, fries, and coleslaw.

CHAPTER TWENTY

James opened the computer file detailing information about Glaxton's in New York. There were twenty entries. Not knowing the murderer's age, first name, or location, he eliminated some over sixty and teens or deceased. He had Violet's description that her abductor was probably in his late thirties and continued scrolling.

Through his open door, a familiar-figured woman entered, Detective Worth, carrying a document.

"Sally, did you find anything on the homeless victim?"

"Yes, James I got a name." She handed the printout over to him.

"Larry Gravina, hmm, who uses medical marijuana. How did you get it?"

"I went to Light of Hope mission in uniform to speed up answers from everyone. A guy actually came up and handed me Gravina's certificate card for obtaining marijuana from legal sources. He didn't know what to do with it now that 'Rigoletto's dead'. Larry had lent it to him before leaving to go to the opera. The dispensary needed an additional form of identification so he told them he'd return with it and went outside. He still had the friend's card."

James thanked her and requested she sit in the chair beside him to view the screen.

"I just found this, Sally. What do you think about this item from Horsehead News?"

> 'A nine year old, Jake Arnold Glaxton, staged a one-person protest at Gravini Landscaping and Excavation. Carrying a sign saying unfair he told reporters that Gravini chopped up the tree containing the tree-house he had builkt and Sniddlee, his favorite pet, a snake. Larry Gravini made no comment except, "It had to be done".'

"Wow" Worth exclaimed. There's the connection between victim and murderer. Suppose it's coincidence we found out both things together? Or it's divine intervention?"

"I never rule out God's help."

"Me either."

James continued, "If we're going to catch this guy, more work is necessary. Would you investigate Horseheads while I focus on tree cutting convention tonight. It's highly probable Glaxton will show up." As Sally went out the door, he watched briefly. Even in police uniform, she was enough to make men dream. Rookies who noticed that and made remarks using her name. 'Worth's worth it' and like innuendos were met with reprimands from protectively indignant Lieutenant James. Her assets extended beyond outstanding physical attributes as those rookies eventually learned.

Anticipating what equipment would be displayed at the convention, James researched types used in the Amazon Rainforest. Environmentalists described some as hellish:

- ***Konrad Highlander*** – muscular testosterone, dripping arm which stretches chasis to climb and fell trees – it's one job to topple trees for pulp.
- ***John Deere 843J*** grips and rips unlike All-American JD tractors that James and others admired
- ***Timberjack Walking Harvester*** chops massive trees down in seconds
- ***Feller Buncher*** skidding and assembling of 2 or more trees

James didn't feel rage in machine descriptions not being very obsessive when it comes to trees. He was opposed to deforestation but trees were renewable resources if replanted properly. The overwhelming anger he felt was for murder. No one had a right to take breath from others. He was determined now to get this guy who's lack of respect and selfish view had killed over and again. He had to be stopped. He lined up police officers and briefed them on tonight's procedures. Sally Worth entered, apologizing for interrupting.

"James, the church in Horseheads, Horseheads Ecumenical Church, had enough interesting records for us."

"Go ahead, Sally. We're finished here with plans for tonight."

"The woman I spoke to there, not the secretary but the one responsible for setting up their website. She was very knowledgeable and emailed everything. Some isn't useful though there's a recording of Glaxton's mom singing that the Sunday School used. It's probably not important that she sang it to get Jake to come out of the tree-house for supper…"

"Wait, no that's good. Make a copy of that and send it to Violet Easton. Tell her to learn it and meet me at the Doubletree Inn at six. That's great, Sally. Thanks."

CHAPTER TWENTY-ONE

Entering the convention center, James almost bumped into the exhibit on display. The massive intimidating tree topper known for "grip and rip" use stood seven feet tall in the entry. On the plaque, the type indicated feller-buncher, described operations which foretold inevitable doom for any and all trees. The giant saw on the front was raised up out of visitor's harms way but still frightening to look at. Further on were smaller machines, harvesters, brush whackers or logstackers, sure to be a hit with fans attending.

James had coordinated with and explained to the convention boss, securing enough black caps and shirts that employees wore, for his men and women. If James felt like Paul Bunyan in faded blue jeans and plaid flannel shirt, he ignored it. The goal to blend in superseded it. Violet, in like attire, sat on a chair very near the podium.

People streamed in, observing the machines or visiting booths set for selling Karl Gruber t-shirts, snacks or bottled water. James estimated 100-150 people in attendance. At 6:50, James thought he'd get a water from the vendor across the room. When he got there, though, the guy manning the booth was nowhere around. It was too close to speech time now anyway, so he joined Violet, siiting on her left. A recording of machines and Rainforest sounds began as Gruber came up to the dais, which was covered in cloth.

He ripped of the covering, reacted, then fired at it from the gun he carried in the belt. The sound of shooting caused running as patrons headed for the only open exit. James and Violet stood and watched the dead rattlesnake fall to the floor.

Even though Karl's job was disturbing to James, he had to admire the man's fast recovery making it a joke and reassuring the crowd it was over and okay to stay.

Several things happened – the convention boss opened up three more exits. Outside the row of sycamore trees was visible. The crowd thinned to about fifty inside. The undercover police ditched

anonymity for shooter protocol. The water vendor returned then looked up nonchalantly and walked to the nearest exit.

James spoke to Karl very quickly, "There's a tree hugger murderer in here and you're his target. Go somewhere else safe and take these two officers with you." He motioned to Hynicki and Gray to guard Karl.

Suddenly Violet shouted, "That's the Rattler Glaxton! That man walking toward the Exit C, James!"

James and Violet ran toward him as Glaxton grabbed a little girl exiting. Her mother fell grabbing at him and called, "Somebody help! That man took my daughter outside!"

Hordes of men sprung to action, chasing the fast abductor. Jake, feeling the pursuit behind him, climbed up the closest tree, the girl in tow. James stopped to ask the mother if she was injured, and then the name of her daughter.

"Ashley."

"We'll find him and get her back. This officer will bring you outside."

"I'm not leaving until she is safe."

Five officers, James, Violet and the overwrought mom looked outside at a line of sycamore trees without seeing either Glaxton or Ashley. Officer Wappel stopped in the grass, shouting, "I see him, sir. Third tree on the left I saw movement. I can take him out with one shot."

"Stand down, officer. If a bullet ricochets off a limb it might strike the girl. Don't fire anybody."

James spoke softly to Ashley.

"Stay there, Ashley, okay, we'll get you down. Good girl."

The sound of guns being drawn was frightening to Ashley's mother so Violet put her arms out to hug her. "What's your name?"

"Marjorie..."

Wappel explained he'd won awards for sharp shooting but James refused to listen to it.

"We're trying another option. If it doesn't work...."

James and Violet stood in front of the tree with Glaxton and Ashley several branches up. James spoke calmly, "I'm a policeman, Ashley, get as far as you can from the man. Don't be obvious though." Of course The Rattler would hear that but it couldn't be helped. James nodded to Violet and she sang out hoping God would hear it and Glaxton, too.

> *'Zaccheus was a wee little man'*
> *A wee little man was he*
> *He climbed up in a sycamore tree*
> *For the Lord he wanted to see*
> *And when the Savior passed that way*
> *He looked up in the treehouse. And He said*
> *Zaccheus you come down*
> *For I'm going to your house today'*

Momentarily nothing happened. Jake felt he'd run as far as he could run and retreated to the safety of the tree from childhood.

Hearing his Mom's voice – whether it was spiritual or insanity, he shouted from the tree, "I'm coming Mom." And Jake swung down from the tree bottom. The whizz of a bullet propelled forward striking Jake and he fell down struck on the right leg.

Officer responded quickly to find the source although at least 15 guns were visible in the crowd outside. Apparently big machine fans are gun enthusiasts too. James trusted Wappel to interview everyone finding that the shooter was not Karl (Hynicki Gray attested) nor any officers. James recalled seeing a woman get up from a shooter kneeling position a short time after The Rattler was struck down. Not believing it could be the familiar woman he recognized, he knew certainly it was. The shooter was—inexplicably—Robin from the Angel Sound Technology office. He asked Wappel to detain her. No one was allowed to leave after a shooting, therefore she was somewhere in the crowd. They took Jake away in an ambulance/police secured vehicle combo.

Majorie, seeing the abductor gone, out of the tree, jumped up on the trunk, climbing arm over arm till she felt Ashley's hand. They reached the ground safely and everyone present clapped. As usual, large crowds gather in hostage situations. Karl was out there, Hynicki and Gray on either side, inviting everyone back inside to hear his talk. Also to enjoy a beverage – on him.

"There goes his gratuity, " James said. Wappel walked up to his boss saying, " I hope you don't mind my saying something now, Lieutenant – but kind of hokie using a song to capture a suspect."

"Maybe no more than claiming sharp shooting is perfect, or without mistakes, I guess."

"Touche, sir."

"I take it you're not a fan of psychology."

"No way, sir."

"Well the gist in this situation – a childhood trauma started this guy in murdering. A good childhood memory cleverly used, brought him down. He's going to prison, finding lots of time to sort out craziness in that mind, no longer a threat for us."

"Then his thinking means he is a child? It'd be very hard to shoot someone in that condition."

"Make no mistake. If the little girl hadn't been up in the tree, I would've said, "Go ahead, shoot. Cause is not the same as condition. Trauma only caused childhood thinking. His condition is murderous adult, see?"

"I think so, sir. Thanks for clarifying it."

"Well I've learned a few things at times from catching criminals."

Marjorie walked over with Ashley holding onto her hand, on the way to their car. James knelt down in front of Ashley and smiled, "You're a very brave girl. May I shake your hand?"

Ashley giggled and put out her hand. "I was scared…, then you spoke. It sounded just like my daddy when I'm upset over something. It helped. Thanks. Can we be friends? I don't have a policeman friend. I'd like to." James smiled, answering yes and giving her an official detective card.

James spotted Robin sitting under a tree and walked over.

"Robin. You're not in trouble. That accurate a shot was unexpected, though."

"What *ever* do you refer to now, Lieutenant James?"

"The gun that brought down The Rattler was in your hands. Do you deny it?"

"I don't. I believed protecting that girl from harm important."

"That's reasonable justification. I also *believe* it. Where did you train for that accuracy?"

"From the local Sportsman's Club. It's funny I joined to meet guys, but found skills instead. My father was a policeman here in New York. I guess I picked up some pointers."

CHAPTER TWENY-TWO

The drama over, the ordinary participants gathered at Nurse Nancy's to enjoy food and beverage. The owner of the bar, Doc Friday, a black man from Jamaica set them up at a table toward the back, heartily welcoming everyone. Violet sat with Tom, Harry next to him on the right, Robin and boss David, nearby. Lieutenant James held out a corner chair for Bitsy and sat on her left. A familiar Bob Marley song played on the jute box. Miss Nancy took drink orders, soda for Harry. The favorite was domestic beer, although Bitsy tried Jamaican Rum. James looked up at her, eyebrows questioning.

"It goes with the territory. Don't worry, be happy, James."

James smiled, not surprised that Bitsy picked up the mood of the bar.

David reached over to Harry, "The music is Marley if you're not hearing that."

Harry immediately sang along , exactly in tune. "I had a cochlear implant two weeks ago," Harry told them. "I'm not sure who arranged it but I'm very grateful. I hear fine."

As everyone congratulated him, James glanced knowingly at Tom who was the kind benefactor. Humbly, Tom didn't admit to it but gave Harry a hug for the success of it.

"I understand more congratulations are in order," James said standing up as Doc Friday poured Jamaican champagne, non-alcoholic into seven fluted glasses.

James recited,
"It was meant to be like in birds of a feather
A rattlesnake brought them together
Wishin joy in Jamaica and fair weather
Long life, Violet and Tom
Happy marriage endeavor"

Another beer round, lots of talking and smiles had everyone feeling great. They placed orders for food and Violet sang Jimmy Cliff version of *I Can See Clearly Now*. When the food arrived, James' usual pickiness with what everything was, was not there and he dug into the Jerk Chicken. Violet, Tom, and David ordered Ackee and Saltfish, the National Jamaican dish and Harry enjoyed Stamp and Go, dried salted cod fritters. Bitsy, eating Run Down (Ha!– it's pickled mackerel in coconut milk). Callaloo, or spinach-like native vegetables, on Robin's plate was very delicious. Tom took a break from eating, casually asking, "Who found out our Jamaican honeymoon destination?"

Robin fidgeted first, then leaned forward boldly saying,

"I found brochures left out on computer room desk. Two and two together type thing."

"It's okay. Honeymoons don't need secrecy, only privacy. Nobody's going to surprise us, I'm sure."

All agreed to it.

"Robin," James said. "Are you registered for police training?"

"Yes, sharp-shooting test is Thursday."

"It should put you over the top for a desirable spot."

"I hope it's true."

"Best of luck."

They finished the meal with Pinch-Me-Rounds or other desserts. James paid for the meal. Tom insisted on leaving a tip.

The jute box, now playing in Harry Belafonte's excellent tones,
"Day-O
Day-O"
They all sang going out the door...
"Daylight Come and Me Wanna Go Home"

EPILOGUE

They met Richard Schwartz, nephew of Bitsy exiting the art gallery next door. Warm greeting ensued and Bitsy took the opportunity to invite Richard to the soiree planned in Belize.

"Richard I own a private island…"

"Not so surprising, Aunt Bitsy, you have abundant riches. Are you hosting a wedding event or perhaps even a mystery murder theme gathering now?"

"Just a vacation destination. I hope you'll be there. Invite a friend too."

"Thanks, I will. Email details. Ciao, Aunt Bitsy."

James also looked forward to vacationing on the private Belize Island. He turned to his endearing soulmate. "Someone asked me if I were stranded on a desert island, what book would I bring? *How to Build A Boat* (or plane). That's from comedian Steven Wright. The one that has collection of sea shells he keeps in beaches everywhere all over the world."

THE END

Find out what happens on the island when an evil muderer joins the guests there.
Murders on Private Island JB Clemmens

www.ingramcontent.com/pod-product-compliance
Lightning Source LLC
LaVergne TN
LVHW020433080526
838202LV00055B/5172